Pony for Three

By C. W. Anderson

Billy and Blaze
Blaze and the Forest Fire
Blaze and Thunderbolt
Blaze and the Gypsies
Blaze Finds the Trail

A Pony for Linda
Linda and the Indians
The Crooked Colt
Pony for Three

Bobcat
High Courage
Salute
Big Red
The Horse of Hurricane Hill
Afraid to Ride

Deep Through the Heart
A Touch of Greatness
Tomorrow's Champion
Thoroughbreds
Heads Up, Heels Down
Sketchbook

Pony for Three

By C. W. ANDERSON

The Macmillan Company

New York · 1958

Library of Congress catalog card number: 58–11298

First Printing

Printed in the United States of America

To Sally, Dougy, and Gail Reeves

Spot was a beautiful pony that was given to three children, Sally, Dougy and Gail. They had wanted a pony for a long time and when they saw him they all loved him.

Sally had wanted a brown pony — and half of the pony was brown. Dougy had wished for a white pony — and half of the pony was white. Gail had hoped for a black pony and the pony's flowing mane was pure black. So they all got their wish.

At first Gail was a little timid about riding and so was Dougy. But when Sally got on Spot's back and the pony went quietly around the pasture they all wanted to ride.

Sally led the pony to a big rock so they could all climb on his back. They were so light Spot did not mind. He was a strong pony—just right for three such small riders.

Round and round they went and Spot seemed to be as happy as the children. They rode him every day and there was never any trouble about whose turn it was. It was always everybody's turn.

After every ride they always patted the pony and told him how fine he was and little Gail always said "Thank you." Then they brought presents of carrots and sugar which Spot liked very much. He was happy in his new home.

When the children were at school Spot would look around for someone to play with. Sometimes he would chase the pigeons that came into his pasture. He liked to see them fly on their swift wings.

A little rabbit lived in the pasture and he and the pony had great fun together. Often they would race but the little rabbit always won.

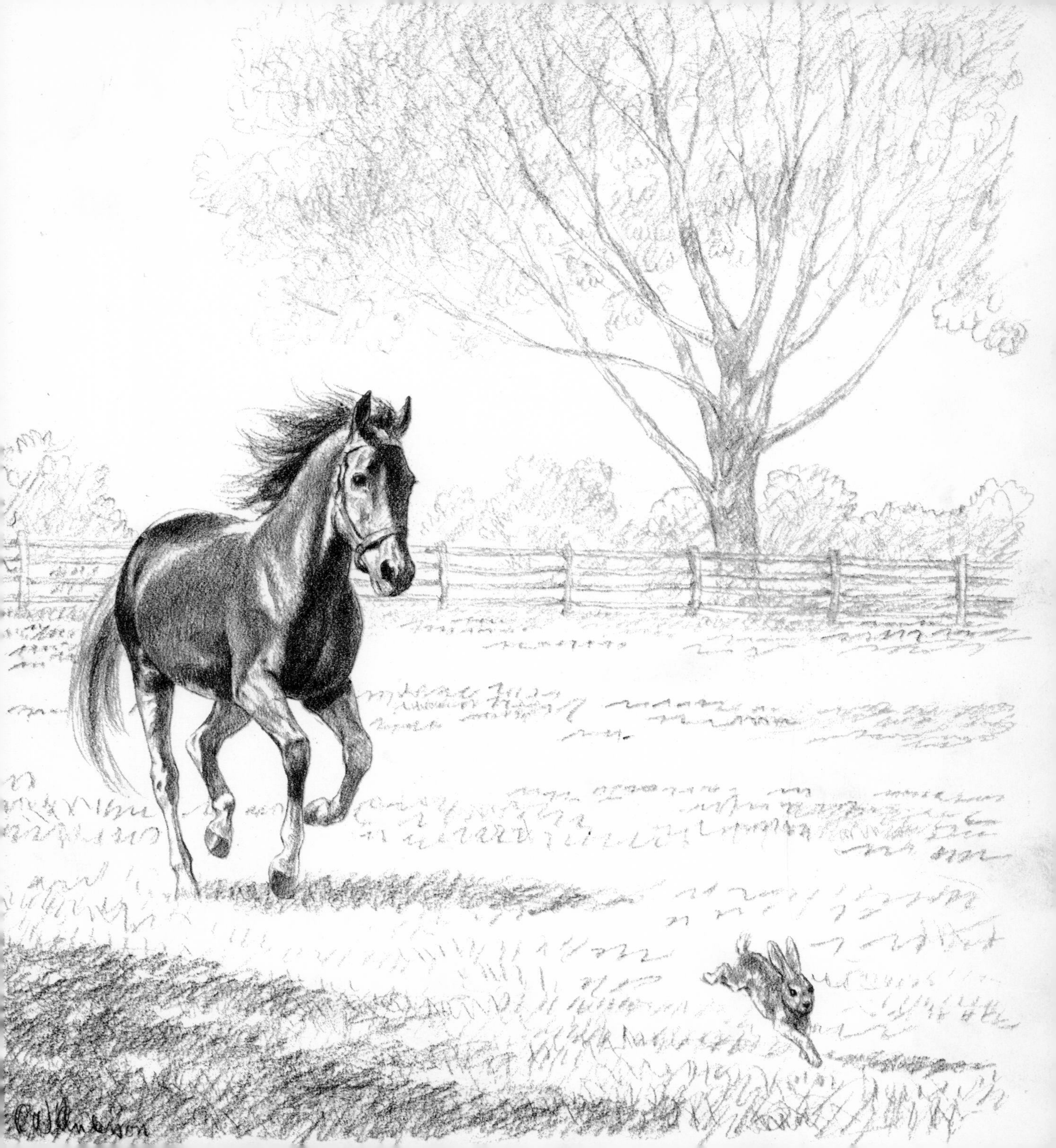

When the rabbit was away Spot would try to play with a gray squirrel that lived nearby. The squirrel did not want to play. He always ran up a tree and sat there and scolded and scolded.

An old woodchuck had his home in the pasture and sometimes the pony pretended to chase him. Spot did not really want to catch him but the fat old woodchuck looked so funny when he ran.

One day Spot was racing with the little rabbit and he almost felt he might win. He was so excited he forgot to watch for the woodchuck's hole in the pasture.

His foot went into the woodchuck hole and over he went with a crash. He knew he was badly hurt and gave a sharp whinny of pain.

The children came running and were very un-happy when they saw Spot could not use one leg. Dougy ran to tell his mother.

Their mother called an animal doctor who came very quickly. He said that the bone in Spot's leg was cracked and he fixed a strong cast for it.

"Take good care of him and keep him quiet and I think he will be all right again," he said.

The children spent all their spare time with their pony. They picked the greenest grass for him so he did not have to walk around. He could not walk well with the stiff cast on his leg.

For weeks they fed and watered him and took the best care of him. He seemed better and happier each day.

At last the doctor came to see the pony again.
When he took off the cast he was pleased.
"I think the leg is well again," he said.

Spot tried the leg carefully and then trotted slowly around the pasture. It seemed fine. All the children were so happy.

"Just let him take it easy for a few days and you can ride him again," said the doctor.

A week went by and Spot seemed very gay and strong. Sally said, "We will try him first with Gail on his back because she is the lightest."

The pony went quietly and seemed happy to be ridden again.

The next day Dougy also climbed on his back and he and Gail rode around the pasture. Spot's leg did not bother him at all.

Then came a day when Sally also climbed on his back and off they went. They were all so happy.

"He is a pony for three again," they said. And he was.